Woollybear Good-bye

STORY BY *Sharon Phillips Denslow*

PICTURES BY *Nancy Cote*

Four Winds Press ⋚⋛ *New York*

Maxwell Macmillan Canada   *Toronto*

Maxwell Macmillan International   *New York   Oxford   Singapore   Sydney*

To Miss Margaret Heath,
who *was* third grade in Benton,
and to Miss Hazel Newton,
and to Dr. L.J. Hortin, who
always believed   —S.D.

To John, my little bug catcher,
and to Missy,
a future Miss Rosemary   —N.C.

The day Joe Dean Castleberry told the class he was
moving to Michigan, Miss Rosemary gave him a hug, told
him she would miss him, and called him a kindred spirit.

Brenda Houser stared at Joe Dean. "You can't
move—school just started."

Curtis Lee frowned and raised his hand. "What
does kindred spirit mean, Miss Rosemary?"

"We're alike, Joe Dean and I," Miss Rosemary said.

The third graders in Miss Rosemary's homeroom looked from Joe Dean to Miss Rosemary. Joe Dean was skinny and had yellow hair that stuck straight up in a cowlick over one eye. He could puff his cheeks out and make sounds like a squirrel, and he ran faster than anyone in class. He was eight years old.

Miss Rosemary had speckled brown hair that she pulled back in a roll. She snapped her fingers and lifted her eyebrows to get their attention, and no one had ever seen her break into a fast trot. Miss Rosemary had been teaching the third grade for twenty-five years. She was too old to tell.

Miss Rosemary smiled at the puzzled third graders. "Joe Dean and I think about things in the same way," she said.

Curtis Lee raised his hand again. "You mean like the rocks?"

"Exactly," Miss Rosemary said.

Miss Rosemary had a rock collection that filled three shelves. Joe Dean added a rock to the collection almost every day.

Brenda didn't care about rocks right now. She wrote a note to Joe Dean. *Why are you moving?* the note said.

Joe Dean wrote back, *My dad's job.*

You're not moving today, are you? wrote Brenda.

Next Saturday, the note said when Joe Dean passed it back.

Miss Rosemary motioned for the class to be quiet. She touched the blackboard, where

FRIDAY'S PROJECT—TURN IN LEAVES

was written in bright yellow chalk.

"Please bring your leaf books to my desk. We'll start with Brenda's row," Miss Rosemary said.

Brenda walked to the front of the room and opened the construction-paper cover to her book.

"Look, Miss Rosemary," she said. "I put my redbud leaf on the first page."

Hands shot up around the room. "I did, too!" "So did I!"
Joe Dean groaned, "My leaves are alphabetical."

"Now, Joe Dean," Miss Rosemary said, "it doesn't matter where
your redbud leaf is as long as it is in your book."

The whole class laughed. Miss Rosemary's redbud grew outside
of the third-grade class windows. It was her favorite tree. She'd
planted it the first day she started teaching. Her classes watered it,
fed it, pruned it, picnicked near it, and drew pictures of it every
spring when it blossomed.

The only thing they were not allowed to do was climb it.

After Miss Rosemary had collected the leaf books, she erased the blackboard. In new red chalk, she wrote

MONDAY'S PROJECT—WOOLLYBEAR WEEK.

Every fall when the black-and-brown woollybear caterpillars began to crawl around looking for hibernation spots, the school celebrated Woollybear Week. Classes made posters and wrote poems about woollybears, and the class that collected the most woollybears got a shiny plaque for its room.

"Now, we need a room 301 Woollybear Week team captain," Miss Rosemary said.

Brenda waved her hand, "I vote for Joe Dean for captain!" she said.

Hands shot up all over the room. The vote was unanimous.

"Joe Dean Castleberry is the official room 301 Woollybear Week Captain," Miss Rosemary announced. "All woollybears must be turned in to Joe Dean by noon on Thursday. Mr. Duke will announce the winning team at our special assembly on Thursday afternoon. Please remember to keep your woollybears in jars or boxes with holes in the lids! Good luck, team 301!"

On Monday, everybody had at least 1 woollybear for Joe Dean. Brenda brought him 5. Curtis Lee had found 8. "I bet I can find more than anyone else," he said.

Joe Dean wrote *45* under the picture of the furry woollybear Miss Rosemary had drawn on the board.

Tuesday it rained, and Curtis Lee was the only one who found a woollybear. It was hiding under a soggy leaf by the bus stop.

Joe Dean reported that the second grade had collected 51 woollybears already. The fourth grade had 48.

The woollybears were out again Wednesday morning, traveling
in the warm sun. Curtis Lee found 3, and other kids turned in 16.
Brenda brought in 2 fat ones. "They were crawling on my
back steps," she said.
Joe Dean wrote 67 on the blackboard.

Most kids shook their heads the next morning when they saw
Joe Dean. Woollybears were getting hard to find.

"We only got 8 today," Joe Dean told the class. He went to
the blackboard and wrote 75 under the chalk woollybear. "The
second grade has 59," Joe Dean announced. "But the fourth
grade has 75, too. We need 1 more woollybear. Recess is our
last chance!"

At recess, the class fanned out so that they could cover every inch of playground. The second and fourth graders had the same idea, and the playground was crowded. But there were no woollybears anywhere.

Brenda wandered over to Miss Rosemary's redbud tree and poked at the leaves on the ground with a stick. She wondered if Joe Dean would like his new school. She wondered if woollybears lived in Michigan, too. Suddenly, Brenda stopped poking leaves and stared at the redbud tree.

There, crawling up the bumpy trunk, was the biggest woollybear she had ever seen. Brenda grabbed the lowest limb and pulled herself up. A woollybear that big would be a fast crawler.

Brenda carefully moved from limb to limb up and up the tree. Miss Rosemary wasn't going to like this. Miss Rosemary did not allow anyone to climb her prize redbud, no matter what.

"Brenda!"

Brenda looked down. Miss Rosemary and Joe Dean and the third graders from room 301 were gathered under the tree watching her.

"I've got our winning woollybear!" she yelled.

Brenda climbed after the woollybear. She finally caught him on one of the top branches, still crawling madly for the sky.

Joe Dean climbed up to the fork in the trunk and cupped his hands around the winning woollybear.

"76," he said happily, just as the end-of-recess bell rang.

At the woollybear assembly that afternoon, each class captain announced their woollybear total. Miss Rosemary's third graders grew quiet when the fourth-grade captain stood up. What if the fourth grade had found another woollybear, too?

"75," announced the fourth-grade captain.

"Room 301 has 76 woollybears!" Joe Dean announced in a clear, proud voice.

"68," said the second-grade captain.

Mr. Duke, the principal, and Miss Daisy, the assistant principal, officially counted the woollybears. Room 301 had 76 exactly. The third graders whooped. They were the winners!

After assembly, Miss Rosemary had a woollybear-shaped cake and a bowl of punch with ice cream floating in it on her desk. A woman from the newspaper came to take Joe Dean's picture, and Miss Daisy took the bronze woollybear plaque into town to have it engraved.

"Your name will be on the plaque in Miss Rosemary's homeroom for ever and ever," Brenda reminded Joe Dean.

On Friday afternoon, just before school let out for the day, the class took the woollybears outside by the redbud tree and turned them loose.

It was time for them to go, and Joe Dean, too.

"That was a brave thing Brenda did yesterday, and I'm proud of room 301," Miss Rosemary said. "But I don't ever want to see any of you climbing my redbud again."

Twenty-two kindred spirits nodded in agreement.

At Thanksgiving time, the class sent Joe Dean a folder
of pressed leaves and drawings.

He sent them a gray-and-pink rock from Lake Michigan
at Christmas.

And in the spring, when the redbud tree blossomed, the
Isabella tiger moths that had once been Joe Dean Castleberry's
winning woollybears filled the air.